B 6-9

QUEST
GANG
GO IN TO ACTION

1991

Presented to

Angus Mackinnon

Arnisort

Sunday School

C.L.C. Bookshops.

© Louis Fidge 1987

ISBN 0 86201 516 2

All rights reserved. No part of this publication may
be reproduced, stored in a retrieval system, or
transmitted, in any form or by any means, electronic,
mechanical, photocopying, recording or otherwise,
without the prior permission of Scripture Union.

Phototypeset by Input Typesetting Limited, London
Printed and bound in Great Britain by
Cox and Wyman Limited, Reading

THE QUEST GANG
GO IN TO ACTION

LOUIS FIDGE

Scripture Union
130 City Road, London EC1V 2NJ

Meet the Quest Gang – Raju, Jake, Sally, Lucy, Julie and Tom. They're six members of the Quest Club at Green Street School.

1

Drums, tambourines and recorders went flying as Tom fell against the music trolley. It tilted dangerously over to one side. Drumsticks and castanets clattered and rolled on the tiled floor. Triangles swung wildly and clashed against each other.

Tom reached for the side of the trolley. He caught hold of the middle bar and just managed to stop the whole thing from falling right over. But as he grabbed it, the big brass cymbal on the top shelf shot off and sailed through the air.

'Look out! U.F.O.s are invading Quest Club H.Q.!' shouted Jake.

Loud clashing sounds filled the hall, echoing and bouncing off the walls. As the clang of the cymbal subsided, silence settled. Everyone froze to the spot. The Quest Gang drew in their breath, hardly daring to move. They weren't sure what to do or how to react.

Jake's smile froze on his face. Raju looked serious. Julie stopped putting the song books away and turned round. She stood like a statue with a startled expression. Sally and Lucy stopped chatting. Sally's mouth was half open in surprise at the unexpected interruption.

Tom could feel himself going red with embarrassment. He felt clumsy and silly. He was painfully aware of everyone staring at him. His heart was beating so loudly that he was sure everyone could hear it.

Mr Crossland broke the silence. 'Well, I reckon that was the best performance of the afternoon! Better than anything you lot have managed so far!'

Everyone was taken by surprise. They had expected Mr Crossland to be annoyed or upset. Instead, he was joking with them! Now that they realized Tom wasn't going to get into trouble, the Gang could relax. Smiles and laughter broke out all around. Everyone started talking excitedly about what had happened.

'Come on! How about giving a hand to clear things up?' suggested Mr Crossland.

He went quietly up to Tom. 'Don't worry. No harm's been done. None of the instruments are damaged. And I'm sure you didn't do it on purpose.'

That was true enough. Tom had been putting his tambourine away when his foot had slipped and he fell against the trolley. Somehow things like that always seemed to happen to him!

Tom really liked Mr Crossland. He was one of his favourite teachers at Green Lane. He was always kind and patient. Tom had never really known his own father. His parents had separated when he was small. Now he and his mum lived on their own in a council flat. Sometimes Tom wished he had a dad like Mr Crossland. Mr Crossland seemed to understand him and know just how he felt.

While Mr Crossland and Tom were talking, the rest of the Quest Club began to tidy up the hall. They did it after every meeting to save Mr Biggs, the caretaker, some work. Mr Biggs could be very grumpy at times. He was always moaning about messy children. In fact he never seemed to be happy unless he had something to complain about! Everyone wanted to make sure that he never had any complaints about the state of the hall after Quest Club meetings.

Quest Club met every Monday evening, straight after school. Everyone came armed with Quest notes and Bible, ready to talk about what they had read during the week. Mr Crossland organized it and the Club members never knew quite what to expect. There might be singing, or drama, or quizzes or a mixture of everything! But it was always great fun.

This week they had been reading part of Matthew's gospel. It was all about how God wants us to help other people. As it was nearly Harvest Celebration, they had been making up their own Harvest song, too.

'It's a good idea to use those musical instruments,' laughed Mr Crossland. 'It drowns your awful singing!'

But he was only joking. Sally and Lucy could sing very well, and Raju was great with the recorder. Jake always thought of himself as a good singer, too, but his sister Julie told him that he sounded like a cracked cement mixer!

The warm September sunlight streamed into the hall as everyone set about tidying up. They were so busy that they didn't notice the hall doors opening. Mrs Crossland's head appeared around the door. She caught her husband's eye and smiled. Mr Crossland waved to her and beckoned her in.

Mrs Crossland was on her way home from shopping and had called to pick up her husband. With her was their ten-month old baby, Jemma. Jemma had thin, blond, curly hair. She was a cheerful baby, always smiling. When she saw all the children, her chubby legs kicked with excitement and her eyes lit up.

Jemma was clutching a half-demolished chocolate biscuit. The mess she was making was unbelievable! She slurped and sucked, dribbled and drooled. Most of the chocolate was over her face. The rest had melted and gone all sticky and gooey between her fingers.

'How on earth will I get you clean?' groaned Mrs Crossland, dabbing at Jemma's face with a tissue.

'If you think Jemma's messy, you should see Julie eat,' said Jake, 'She's worse than a chimp at a monkey's tea party.'

Julie wasn't going to stand for that. She grabbed at Jake, but he was too quick. He saw her coming and made a dash for safety. A mad chase started, dodging in and out of everyone. Julie desperately tried to catch Jake while the rest of the group shouted their encouragement. Jemma bounced up and down waving her arms in the air. She was enjoying every bit of it.

'O.K. you lot, calm down or we'll be in trouble with Mr Biggs for making such a fuss,' joked Mr Crossland. 'Let's gather round for a minute before we go.'

Julie glared at Jake as the group gradually quietened and gathered round Mr and Mrs Crossland.

'Just you wait, Jake. I'll get you for that,' muttered Julie.

Jake grinned and made sure he was well out of her way, just in case! She'd have to wait a while before she got the chance to pay her brother back.

'We'll finish with a prayer,' said Mr Crossland.

Everyone closed their eyes and waited.

'Father God, thank you. . .'

'Hic!' interrupted Jemma.

Sally and Lucy glanced at each other and giggled.

'. . .for all the food you give us.'

'Hic!'

'Help us not to waste it. Amen.'

'Amen' said the Quest Club.

'Hic!' said Jemma.

'See you in the morning,' smiled Mr Crossland. 'Take care crossing that main road. And don't forget to let me have any good ideas for the Harvest Celebration. Off you go, then.' He ruffled Tom's hair as he passed by. 'No more accidents, eh?'

Tom grinned.

'Oh! I nearly forgot! I brought something for you all,' called Mrs Crossland. She reached under her chair and pulled out a plastic carrier bag full of apples. 'I picked them from the tree in our garden. I hope you like them.'

'Great! Yeah, thanks,' murmured the group in appreciation.

The hall echoed with the sound of champing and chomping. Apple-filled mouths called out their thank-yous and goodbyes as the children straggled down the path to the main gate.

Mr Crossland bent down to pick up Jemma.

'Now to get you home and into the bath, young lady.'

He lifted her and tossed her up and down in the air. Jemma giggled and squealed...and dribbled chocolate all over his jacket!

Mr Crossland made up this wordsearch for the Quest Club. It's based on the Bible passage Matthew 25:31-40. There are nine words hidden in it. Find the words and cross them out.

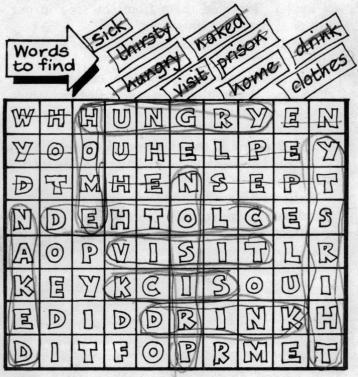

Words to find → sick thirsty naked hungry visit prison home drink clothes

W	H	H	U	N	G	R	Y	E	N
Y	O	O	U	H	E	L	P	E	Y
D	T	M	H	E	N	S	E	P	T
N	D	E	H	T	O	L	C	E	S
A	O	P	V	I	S	I	T	L	R
K	E	Y	K	C	I	S	O	U	I
E	D	I	D	D	R	I	N	K	H
D	I	T	F	O	P	R	M	E	T

Write out the left over letters to discover something Jesus said to his friends.

When you helped these people you did it for me.

2

The kitchen door burst open. Jake and Julie tumbled breathlessly in. Mrs Martin looked up from cooking tea and smiled.

'Hello you two. How was school today?'

'Not bad,' replied Julie.

'Mmmm. That smells good. What's for tea?' Jake asked. He peered past his mum into the frying pan.

'Your favourite-beefburger and chips,' Mrs Martin answered. 'We're having tea early tonight. Dad's working late and I've got to pop round to see Grandpa. He's hurt his back working at the allotment. I keep telling him not to do so much but he's as stubborn as a mule!'

Jake tried to pinch a chip but his mum spotted him.

'Hey! No chips before you've washed and changed,' she laughed. 'Now hop it you two! Tea's in a couple of minutes.'

Julie and Jake clattered up the stairs, pushing and bumping each other as they went.

When they came down Mrs Martin was just serving up the beefburgers. Golden brown chips were already on the plates.

'Jake - dish up the beans, will you?' his mum asked.

In no time at all the children were sitting in the front room, with trays on their laps, tucking into their tea. Julie had switched on Newsround. Jake had his nose buried in his new football comic.

'Can I leave you to do the washing up?' Mrs Martin asked as she put her coat on.

'Yes sure,' mumbled Jake. 'Julie won't mind, will you Julie?'

'Well in that case, you can dry up, can't you?' smiled Mrs Martin. Jake groaned. He thought he'd managed to get away with it but there was no escape.

'I won't be long. And don't fight while I'm out, will you? Be good. Bye for now. See you later.'

The front door clicked shut behind her. Mrs Martin's footsteps became fainter as she hurried down the front path.

Jake got up and cut himself a chunk of cake. He settled back down to his comic. But Julie was engrossed in Newsround. They were showing a report from part of Africa which had been badly

hit by famine.

'Oh Jake, look at that. It's horrible.' Julie dug Jake with her elbow. She pointed at the TV. 'Look-that baby's just a bag of bones!'

Jake grunted and continued to read his comic. 'Look, look,' Julie persisted. There was something in her tone of voice which made Jake look up.

The reporter was talking while a film of the famine was being shown.

'There is a terrible shortage of water and food. Money is desperately needed if the situation is to be helped.'

The pictures were horrifying. Children were starving to death. They were just lying, motionless, waiting to die. Mothers held their babies close, crying to themselves. They had no milk or food to give them.

Jake suddenly felt guilty. His mouth was full of cake and his stomach was full of beefburger and chips. Julie's mind flashed back to baby Jemma. She was chubby, happy and well looked after. Jemma never went hungry. Suddenly Julie remembered what they'd been talking about in Quest Club.

'Jake - we've got to do something. Do you remember this afternoon? We read that bit where Jesus said 'I was hungry and you gave me something to eat, I was thirsty and you gave me something to drink.' Those people are hungry and thirsty. What can we do to help?' Julie asked.

Jake put his comic down and thought for a moment.

'You're right - we ought to do something. But what?'

'How about talking to the rest of the Gang?' suggested Julie.

'Yeah. I bet we could come up with all sorts of ideas,' said Jake excitedly. 'Let's ring them now.' He wanted to get the Quest Gang into action as soon as possible.

'Mum and Dad are out. The Gang could meet up here,' said Julie. 'I'll phone them now.'

As she jumped up, her elbow accidentally caught Jake's arm and rammed the remainder of his cake into his mouth. Jake was left spluttering and choking as Julie raced towards the phone.

3

The rest of the Quest Gang lived fairly close, so within minutes they arrived at Jake and Julie's house. They made themselves comfortable, lying scattered all over the living room. The girls lay side by side on their stomachs on the carpet. Jake and Raju sprawled on the settee, whilst Tom was curled up in Mr Martin's favourite armchair. Julie and Jake's dog, Scruff, was having a great time. He knew something unusual was happening. He sensed excitement in the air. He couldn't settle and kept getting up and wandering about, sniffing and stepping over the girls, licking every hand that stroked him. Eventually he plonked himself down in his usual place on the sheepskin rug in front of the gas fire.

Jake cleared his throat. 'Julie and I thought we'd call a meeting tonight because we saw something on the Newsround that really upset us. We wanted to talk about it to see if there's anything we could do to help.'

'Do you mean that bit about the starving people in Africa?' asked Sally.

'Yes, that's the bit,' replied Jake.

'I didn't see it. What was it all about?' asked Tom.

'Oh, it was really horrible,' said Lucy. 'There were pictures of people who hadn't got any food. They were starving to death.'

'The reporter said it's because of the drought. They haven't had any rain for ages in some places and they can't grow any food,' added Raju.

'I think the whole thing is horrible. We've got loads to eat and drink. Can't we all do something to help?' Jake suddenly asked. Heads nodded in approval and agreement. Scruff opened his eyes, and snorted, his tail twitching swiftly as if to say he thought so too!

'Yes, let's do something,' agreed Julie, 'But . . . what?'

'I know!' exclaimed Tom. He shouted so excitedly that Scruff's eyes snapped open in surprise. He leapt to his feet, his tail swishing from side to side as if he were a helicopter about to take off!

'If these people need food - let's send them some! My mum's got a cupboard full of food.' He paused for a moment and then added, 'I could send all the things I don't like, then I wouldn't have to eat them! I hate tinned peas and we've got dozens

of tins of them at home I could give away.'

'Yeah, what a great idea,' joined in Lucy. 'My mum always makes me eat corned beef just because my dad likes it. I know for a fact we've got three cans of it at home. I could send two of them.'

'What about sending sprouts?' added Julie.

'Or cabbages,' suggested Sally.

Suddenly everyone was mentioning the food they didn't like eating.

'I'll send mushrooms.'

'And rice pudding.'

'And fish.'

'And prunes.'

'Hang on a minute,' said Jake. 'It's no good sending things like that. They'd be rotten before they got there.'

'And tins would cost a lot to send. Could we afford the postage?' asked Raju.

'And even if we could afford it, where would we send them to?' added Sally.

The atmosphere of excitement was evaporating. It wasn't going to be as easy to help as the Gang had first thought. Silence slowly settled as the enormity of the problem began to dawn on them.

Eventually Raju spoke. 'They need more than just food, don't they? They all looked so ill. They must need doctors and nurses to help them get better.'

'And proper homes to live in, and clean water to drink,' added Sally.

'I hadn't thought about all that,' said Lucy. 'It's a much bigger problem than it seemed.'

'But they looked so poor,' said Julie. 'How can they pay for those things if they haven't got money?'

'I've got it!' exclaimed Jake. 'All the things we've been talking about cost money. And raising money is something we are good at isn't it? Remember the fund raising we did at Quest Club to help the blind? We made lots of money. We could easily do it again.'

The whole group suddenly caught the excitement of Jake's idea.

'That's a great idea, Jake,' said Raju.

'Yeah, let's send money.'

'But where would we send it?' asked Sally.

'Don't worry, Sally. There's bound to be lots of organizations who are working in Africa. I bet Mr Crossland would know about them if we asked him,' replied Jake. He went on, 'Right! We all seem to think raising money's a good idea so let's think about the sort of things we could do.' Jake liked to get things planned and organized.

'How about a shoe cleaning squad? There must be thousands of pairs of shoes in the area that need cleaning,' suggested Raju.

'And think of all the babies,' added Lucy.

'I don't fancy cleaning babies. They make a real mess,' said Tom, remembering the state Jemma had got herself into earlier that day.

Lucy laughed. 'I don't mean cleaning them. I mean helping to look after them, you twit.'

'Oh, I see,' said Tom feeling a bit silly.

'What about sponsored events? They're good for raising a lot of money. Remember how much Mr Crossland raised when we sponsored him to shave off his beard,' said Julie.

'It's a shame you haven't got a beard,' teased Jake, straight away.

'Ha, ha. Stop trying to be funny and be serious for a change,' snapped Julie. She'd had enough of Jake's teasing for one day. 'How about you thinking of something?'

'How about a sponsored silence?' replied Jake, quick as a flash. 'I'd like to see you keep quiet for a few hours.' Julie glared angrily at him. 'Oh dear,' thought Jake. 'I've really gone and done it now!' 'Sorry Julie, I was only joking,' Jake said. 'I didn't mean to get at you. If you don't like the idea of a sponsored silence, how about a sponsored marathon, like they have on the telly?'

'Oh no,' groaned Sally. 'That's no fun. That's more like torture. How about a sponsored horse ride? I'd join in that.' Sally loved horses. She was always getting books out of the library on horses, reading stories about horses, and was forever drawing them.

The Gang talked enthusiastically for a while. Everyone had ideas they wanted to add. All the noise got a bit much for Scruff. He couldn't stand the excitement a moment longer. He jumped onto the settee between Jake and Raju. Jake grabbed his collar and rolled about playfully.

Suddenly the room became chaotic. Jake and Scruff fell off the settee onto the girls. They leapt for cover, banging into Tom and Raju. Everyone began to get noisy and excited.

No-one noticed the click of the front door as Mrs Martin let herself in. She stood and looked in surprise at the scene in her front room. Surely there had only been two children and a dog when she went out.

'Jake, Julie? What's going on?'

Jake explained what they had been doing. His mum listened quietly, nodding and smiling.

'Well, that sounds really good. But just look at the time. You've done enough talking for one night. I think you'd all better be off home before it gets dark. It's school tomorrow don't forget,' added Mrs Martin. 'You can talk about your ideas there.'

The Gang groaned. They'd forgotten it was Monday. 'Go straight home, mind. No dawdling or talking to strangers,' said Mrs Martin as the Gang stood up and hunted for their coats.

Jake and Julie went to the front door to see their friends off. There were waves and shouts of 'See you at school in the morning.' Jake and Julie watched as Raju and Tom, and Lucy and Sally disappeared down the road still talking excitedly about what they could do.

The Quest Gang could use some more ideas! Can you help them out?

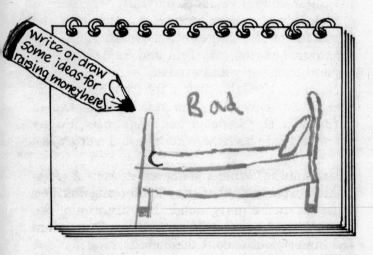

Now read on to see if the Gang have used any of your suggestions.

4

Break time couldn't come quickly enough. As soon as they were let out of class, the Gang huddled together in the playground. The urgency of the previous night was still with them. They were talking excitedly about their ideas.

Mr Crossland was on playground duty. He spotted the Gang and strolled over to find out what was going on.

'Are you lot planning to blow up the school or something?' joked Mr. Crossland. 'What on earth are you up to?'

They all started to chatter at once. 'Whoe! Hold on a minute. One at a time. You first, Julie,' Mr Crossland said.

Julie quickly explained about Newsround and their idea to raise money for Africa. Mr Crossland nodded.

'We saw that report on the news last night, too.

My wife is going to knit up odds and ends of wool into blankets and vests to send out there.'

'I thought Africa was hot,' said Tom.

'Yes it is in the daytime, but it can get very cold at night,' explained Mr Crossland.

'That's something you could do then, Tom,' said Jake. 'You're a bit of a nit!' Everyone laughed except Tom. He didn't think it was funny.

'What ideas have you had so far?' asked Mr Crossland, 'Don't expect me to shave off my beard again for you. It's only just beginning to grow back after the last time!'

'We've already thought of lots of ways to raise money but we're not sure where to send it,' Raju said.

'Oh, that's no problem. I can help you with that. I'll give you the names of plenty of organizations. Now, how about telling me your money-raising plans?' suggested Mr Crossland.

Lucy had just launched into an explanation when a scuffle broke out on the other side of the playground.

'Excuse me — I'd better be off,' muttered Mr Crossland. 'It looks like there's another problem to solve. I'll talk with you later.'

'How about deciding what we're going to do right now!' suggested Sally.

'Well I fancy something to do with sport,' Jake put in straightaway.

'How about a sponsored run, then?' asked Tom. Everyone groaned.

'I know – a sponsored football game,' said Jake. This didn't meet with approval from Sally or Lucy although Julie quite fancied the idea.

'I know!' exclaimed Raju. 'I've got just the thing – a sponsored bike ride!'

Jake's face lit up. 'Great idea! I'd really enjoy that,' said Jake. 'We could go to Ashridge and back.'

The girls didn't seem too enthusiastic but Tom fancied joining in. He was bike mad. He was hopping up and down with excitement. 'Can I come too?' he asked eagerly.

Jake looked at him. He didn't want Tom tagging along. 'I don't know, Tom. There's a lot of main roads on the route – and you haven't passed your cycling proficiency test, have you?'

Tom mumbled that he hadn't.

Jake looked over Tom's shoulder to Raju.

'It'll be a bit dangerous, Tom. I don't think you'd better come – just to be on the safe side,' added Raju.

Tom's face fell. He desperately wanted to go, but it was clear that Jake and Raju weren't going to let him.

Julie felt sorry for Tom. She wondered what she could do to make him feel better. She racked her brains for an idea. Suddenly it came.

'Car washing!' Julie blurted out loudly.

Everyone stopped talking and looked at her. 'Well, most people have got cars,' she went on, 'I bet there's lots of people like my dad. He hates washing the car.'

'I'll stick with the bike ride thanks,' replied Jake, wrinkling his nose.

'Me too,' added Raju.

The idea of sloshing about with water appealed to Tom.

'I'll help you, Julie' he said.

'Great!' smiled Julie.

'Well that's four of us sorted out. What about you two?' asked Raju looking at Lucy and Sally. 'What are you going to do?'

The problem was that Lucy and Sally couldn't seem to agree. When Lucy suggested something, Sally didn't want to do it. And when Sally suggested something, Lucy didn't want to do it. In the end they were beaten by the bell.

'Why don't we just do anything we're asked to?' said Sally.

'Yes, that seems the best idea,' agreed Lucy.

Then just as they were going into class Lucy had a brainwave. 'Let's call ourselves Odd Jobs Unlimited,' she said.

'Great!' agreed Sally.

All further conversation came to a halt as they filed back inside, but the excitement was still there. All six of them had worked out their plans. Now they had to put them into action.

The Quest Gang are all ready to go! But who are you going to join first?

Jake and Raju's bike ride starts on page 33.

Join Lucy and Tom washing cars on page 51.

Do some odd jobs with Lucy and Sally on page 69.

5

All week Raju and Jake prepared for their bike ride. The first job was to collect sponsors from everywhere they could – school, church, friends and relatives. By the end of the week they had an impressive collection of names.

The two boys got their bikes ready. They cleaned and oiled them, checked the brakes and pumped up the tyres. The route was discussed and planned and marked on a map.

At last Saturday came. Just before 9 o'clock, Jake arrived at Raju's house and rang the door bell.

'All set then?' he asked as Raju opened the door.

As usual, Jake was wearing his England Team T-shirt and shorts. He carried a small back pack containing his sandwiches and a can of drink. His mum had made him put in a plastic cagoule, too, in case it rained. She had also got him to take a first aid tin with plasters and antiseptic cream.

'What a fuss,' thought Jake.

'Come on, let's go! I've been ready for ages. I've got the map,' replied Raju.

Mr and Mrs Sharma came out to see them off, followed by Nila, Raju's little sister. She was waving her breakfast spoon in the air. Mrs Sharma gave Raju his packed lunch and slipped a 10p coin into his hand.

'We'll be at home all day, so ring if you get into difficulties. And mind how you go.'

'Course we will,' said Raju, moving quickly out of the door. He wanted to avoid his mum, who was advancing rapidly towards him threatening to smother him with a hug. Jake smiled. He'd had

exactly the same trouble with his own mum!

'Right, we're off!'

With no further ado, Jake and Raju jumped on their bikes and started to pedal. As they reached the end of the road they looked back over their shoulders and waved.

The worst part of the ride was going along the main road. Huge lorries and buses thundered past, making the boys wobble in their slip streams. They were both secretly glad when they turned off into the quieter country lanes.

The route was fairly flat until they got to Hunters Hill. Its steepness proved to be quite a test for their stamina. They were both puffing and gasping breathlessly by the time they got to the top. They didn't actually stop till they arrived hot and sweating at Ashridge village some time later.

'Time to eat, I reckon,' said Raju.

The boys fished their sandwiches out of their bags and tucked into them ravenously.

'It's funny how hungry you get when you've done some exercise,' said Jake, munching his marmite and cucumber sandwiches.

'Here, have one of these,' said Raju, offering Jake one of his salt and vinegar crisps. In return Jake swapped him one of his cheese and onion ones. Crunching replaced the conversation for a while.

Jake shook his can of fizzy drink and tugged at the ring pull. It frothed and hissed and squirted noisily in all directions. Raju and Jake were both splattered with sticky liquid.

'Hey, watch it Jake. This isn't the best place to take a shower,' laughed Raju.

Jake took a long swig of his fizzy drink and burped loudly. 'That's better!' he said. 'Mind you, I'd have got a right telling off if I'd done that at home!'

'Me too,' said Raju, gulping down the last dregs of his drink. He matched Jake's burp with an equally loud reply. Raju looked around guiltily to see if anyone had heard, and he was relieved to find no one in sight.

Jake pretended to have superhuman strength and with a great show of effort, slowly crumpled his empty can with one hand. 'Wow!' exclaimed Raju, in mock admiration. 'What a hero!'

Jake tossed the can into the air and dived at it headlong. He nodded the 'ball' with his head towards the trunk of the tree. 'And Jake Martin, England centre forward, scores another brilliant goal with his head. He's left the goalkeeper stranded. The crowd are going mad with excitement' Jake said in his best sports commentator's voice.

Raju raced to the can and flicked it into the air with his foot. For the next couple of minutes the two boys enjoyed a rough and tumble impromptu game of football.

They soon became hot and sticky again. They

sat down to rest and began chatting about the ride.

'We made pretty good time but I think we could do it even quicker on the way back,' Jake said. 'I noticed a short cut through the woods just before Hunters Hill. I bet that would save us at least ten minutes cycling.'

'I saw that too. Weren't there two footpaths starting at the same place? Let's get out the map and have a look,' suggested Raju.

He rummaged in his bag and pulled out the map. They settled down and studied it closely until they found the spot.

'Yes, you're right, Raju. Look. There *are* two footpaths – but which one's the best?' asked Jake.

The boys peered intently at the map and traced both paths with their fingers. Jake's short cut followed a footpath through Bluebell Woods and would take about a mile off their journey. Raju's path ran round the outside of the wood, crossing a small stream that was marked on the map.

'Well, they both look promising. It's difficult to tell which would be best just by looking at the map. Let's decide when we get there,' suggested Raju.

Little did they know that the homeward journey would be a lot more eventful than the first part!

* * *

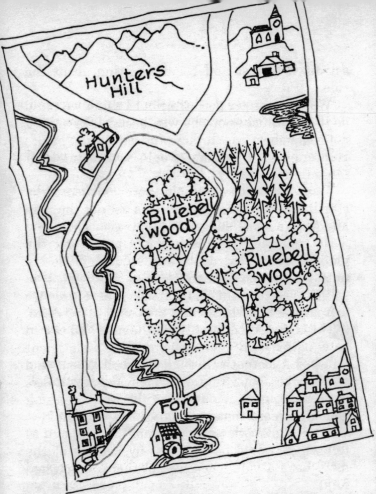

There are two ways back from Bluebell Woods.
Spin a coin to see which way you are going to
follow. If it lands heads up, follow Jake's path. If
it lands tails up, follow Raju's path. (But you can
always read about the other way later!)

Jake's route

Jake and Raju stood where the two paths forked, and tried to decide which one to take. Eventually Jake spoke.

'How about taking the path through the woods? I'm hot and that way looks nice and cool.'

'Yeah. That's fine with me', answered Raju, who also favoured a bit of shade. 'Let's go!'

The boys pedalled towards the wood. They sped down the path, freewheeling along to where the trees started.

At first the path was fairly wide. It had bushes, tall grass and occasional nettles growing alongside. Branches of trees overhung their route creating a sort of tree tunnel effect. Patches of sunlight streamed through.

'Those sun beams look just like rays from a laser gun, don't they?' remarked Raju, pointing to them.

'I will exterminate you', replied Jake in his best Dalek voice, pointing a make-believe laser gun at Raju.

After a while the path got narrower. It dropped away sharply on one side, forming a sort of overgrown ditch. The other side sloped slightly upwards. It was also a bit greasier in places where it had got wet with rain and hadn't dried up properly.

'We'd better ride single file,' suggested Raju.

'OK' said Jake, 'I'll go ahead.'

So Jake took the lead and before long he'd turned their ride into an adventure. He imagined himself fighting his way through an uncharted jungle. As Jake hacked at the overhanging branches with his hand, he pretended he was using a machette to chop his way through dense creepers.

'Keep your eyes skinned for cannibals!' joked Raju.

They pretended that the wood was full of head hunting natives, lying in wait, ready to pounce on any unsuspecting explorer who happened to be passing. Jake let rip an ear splitting Tarzan impression.

'Aaaagh!' he shouted at the top of his voice, beating his chest with one hand. 'Me – Tarzan

Tarzan not afraid of head hunters or poison darts!'

He turned to look at Raju. Unfortunately he did not notice a particularly low overhanging branch just in front of him! Nor did he notice that the path turned slightly to the right. Raju suddenly realized what was about to happen.

'Look out!' he yelled.

Too late!

Raju slammed on his brakes. He looked on, unable to do anything to save his friend from what happened next.

The branch of the overhanging tree caught Jake across the chest. He was taken completely by surprise. As he only had one hand on his handlebars he could not control the bike. He was knocked off balance. He careered along, wobbling unsteadily in an effort to stop himself from being thrown off. But it was no good. As the path curved away to the right, Jake's rear wheel skidded uncontrollably on a muddy patch and spun from beneath him. Jake felt himself going. The front wheel dipped off the path to the side.

'Help' he yelled at the top of his voice.

Raju watched in disbelief and horror as both Jake and his bike disappeared off the path and went crashing down into the ditch.

Jake seemed to lose contact with the ground. The earth and sky spun round and round like a crazy spinning top. The sun blurred against the trees as it sped by. It was a most peculiar feeling when, for a moment, his bike seemed to be on top of him in the air. Jake saw the bushes at the bottom of the ditch rushing up to meet him.

There was a sickening crash and thud as Jake's body hit the ground. His bike came crashing down on top of him. For a moment his mind went blank, and a thousand stars exploded in his head. Jake groaned. He felt quite dizzy and sick. Sweat broke out on his forehead. He opened his eyes slowly. He had landed in the middle of a bush at the bottom of the ditch, with his bike on top of him. The front wheel was still slowly spinning around. As he looked up he could see Raju's worried face peering down from the path.

'Jake! Jake! Are you all right?' Raju called anxiously. In spite of his pain Jake could still manage a joke. 'No. I'm half left you twit! Come on – get down here and give me a hand!'

Raju scrambled down the slope towards Jake. He tried hard to cheer him up as he did so.

'That was great. What are you going to do for your next trick?' he asked, Raju untangled Jake's bike and lifted it off. He began checking it over for damage.

'Well, your bike looks OK, except for a couple of broken spokes. The front wheel looks a bit bent, too, but I think it'll be all right to get you home,' he said.

'Don't worry about my blooming bike. What about me! Just get me up will you!' exclaimed

Jake impatiently, holding out his hand.

Raju bent over and pulled Jake up. Jake struggled to his feet, drawing in his breath painfully as he put his weight on his right leg. He grabbed hold of Raju's arm as a fresh wave of dizziness swept over him. He closed his eyes for a moment till it passed.

Gingerly Jake began to feel himself to see what damage he'd done. He had a few minor scratches, and quite a nasty cut on his arm which had started bleeding.

'Pity about your shirt,' Raju said, pointing to a big tear at the front. Jake looked down in disappointment. His England shirt was his pride and joy. He seemed more concerned about his T shirt than he was about himself.

Raju suddenly giggled. 'You don't half look a mess.'

'Gosh, my mum'll moan when she sees the state of me,' Jake groaned. He limped up and down a few paces, relieved to be able to put a bit of weight on his right leg. It still hurt, but at least it wasn't broken.

'You've probably just twisted it badly,' suggested Raju as Jake put his arm round his shoulder for support. 'It's jolly lucky you landed on that bush, or you'd have hurt yourself even more,' he added.

'I'd better patch you up,' said Raju dipping into Jake's bag to find the plasters.

'It's funny how mums can sometimes be quite useful isn't it?' said Jake as Raju pulled out the first aid tin that Mrs Martin had made him bring.

A few minutes later Raju stood back and admired his handiwork. Jake looked as though he'd been fighting a war all by himself, but he was beginning to get his breath back. He was still feeling very battered, bruised and shaken but realized he hadn't broken anything. Remarkably the bike had escaped too much damage as well and was still rideable.

Raju dragged Jake's bike up the bank to the path and then came back down to help Jake up. 'I thought you said we'd save time by coming this way?' asked Raju with a twinkle in his eye. 'Are you still glad we took this path?'

The two boys laughed and mounted their bikes, Jake rather more painfully than Raju. They cycled off slowly. Jake decided not to do any more Tarzan impressions on the way home.

Although he felt worse for wear, Jake managed to make it home without any further mishaps. Mind you they had some explaining to do when they got back eventually. But when they thought of all the money they'd raised, it made all their problems seem worth it. In fact their sponsored bike ride had proved to be quite an adventure! And they certainly made the most of it when they told the story to the rest of the gang a bit later!

Raju's route

Jake and Raju stood and looked at the two paths, trying to decide which one to take.

Eventually Raju said, 'That path through the woods looks a bit overgrown. We might not be able to get through that way. How about following the route around the outside?'

'Yeah. That's fine with me,' answered Jake. 'Let's go!'

The two boys leapt onto their bikes and set off at a cracking pace. They had great fun weaving between the large stones that were scattered along the path, avoiding the overhanging branches that hung down from the trees in the woods.

After a few minutes they reached the stream that had been marked on the map. It was fairly shallow and slow running. The water looked clear, cool and inviting.

'I could do with a paddle,' said Raju, who was beginning to feel quite hot.

'Why? Where's your canoe?' joked Jake with a mischievous grin.

The boys stopped and looked at the water longingly.

'Come on, we haven't got time to stop,' said Jake.

'Hey – look at the way we've got to cross over,' exclaimed Raju. His eyes lit up as he looked at a tree trunk which had been laid across the stream as a sort of bridge. It looked good fun. Jake got very excited. What an opportunity for an imaginary adventure! He was determined to be first across.

Jake started speaking as if he were a TV commentator reporting on some important event.

'And as the sun beats down mercilessly, Jake Livingstone, jungle adventurer, prepares himself to cross the raging torrents of the Amazon River. Only a narrow rope bridge spans the river and stands between him and the safety of the other side. Man eating crocodiles infest the water, eyeing Jake hungrily, waiting for the tiniest slip. Will he plummet to a bloody, painful death or will the intrepid explorer beat both the river and the crocodiles and cheat death? Do not take your eyes off this screen. You are about to see history in the making.'

With that Jake bumped his bike up onto the log, gave a carefree wave and wobbled across. He let out an ear splitting 'Yippee' as he successfully reached the side.

'Come on Raju! What's keeping you back?' challenged Jake.

'There's nothing to it – I'll show you how it's done, retorted Raju. His bike gathered speed and rose full tilt at the log.

Unfortunately his approach to the bridge wasn't quite straight and as the front wheel hit the log it jumped to one side and skidded off.

Raju was going too fast to stop and found himself somersaulting head over heels over the handlebars through the air. His bike followed.

It was a strange sensation. The whole world seemed to spin and turn upside down as Raju landed with a splosh in the water. The water frothed and foamed as he splashed about, stirring up mud and pebbles from the bottom. When his head emerged from the water it was crowned by green slimey weeds. He looked like a monster from a horror film.

Jake doubled up with laughter on the other bank. 'Oh come on Raju – stop mucking about. You know we haven't got time for a swim!'

Raju spluttered and shook himself, water

cascaded off him. He was drenched through and through. 'Well at least I'm lovely and cool. Why don't you come in?' joked Raju.

'Look out!' Jake shrieked suddenly – pointing wildly behind Raju with fear in his eyes. Raju spun round. 'Mind the crocodiles don't bite you!'

Raju grinned when he realized he'd been taken in by Jake's teasing. 'I'll get my own back on that smarty pants,' Raju thought to himself. He called out to Jake 'Come on – give me a hand out will you?'

As Jake leaned forward, Raju hit the water with the flat of his hand, making it splash up right into Jake's unsuspecting face. Jake spluttered and laughed at being caught out by his friend.

'Just look at the mess I'm in,' said Raju as he clambered out of the water with his bike. 'My mum'll murder me when I get home.'

Jake was just about to answer when he heard a slow hissing sound coming from Raju's front tyre.

'Oh no! I think you've got a puncture too!' he said. Both boys bent to examine the wheel. Sure enough the tyre was going flat.

'It must have got a puncture as I hit the log,' exclaimed Raju. 'It's lucky I remembered to bring a few tools and a puncture repair outfit along,' he added.

'At least the sun's shining,' said Jake trying to

think of something encouraging to say. 'Come on, let's get on with it.'

The two boys set about fixing the puncture. Fortunately they were both quite good at practical things and within twenty minutes the tyre was mended and they were ready to get going again.

'Well, we didn't save any time by coming this way' said Jake with a twinkle in his eye. 'I bet it would have been quicker to go through the wood!'

They remounted their bikes and cycled off slowly. The journey back helped Raju to dry out gradually and they managed to make it home again without any further mishaps.

Mind you, Raju did have some explaining to do when his mum found weeds in his jeans pocket! But the thought of all the money they'd successfully raised made verything seem worthwhile. In fact, their sponsored bike ride had been quite an adventure! And they certainly made the most of it when they told the story to the rest of the gang.

6

Tom and Julie had planned their day carefully. Together they wrote a list of people (mostly neighbours and friends) who had agreed to let them wash their cars on Saturday. Tom was going to look after the money they collected. His mum had recently given him a large metal money box with a key for his birthday. Julie got together all the equipment for washing the cars. She and her mum had decided that they would need a bucket for the water, some washing up liquid, sponges and cloths and a hose pipe.

Tom had got his own breakfast that morning. His mum worked part time in the local supermarket on the checkout and left early for work. But before she went, she gave him instructions to wear his old clothes. Car washing was bound to be a messy business!

Tom walked his bike round the side of Julie's

house and knocked on the kitchen door. Almost immediately Scruff started barking and pressed his nose against the glass of the kitchen door.

Mr Martin wasn't working this weekend. He opened the door and let Tom in.

'Hello Tom, good to see you. How's it going?' he asked in his friendly voice.

'Oh fine thanks,' Tom replied. 'Is Julie ready?'

Mrs Martin came into the kitchen carrying some cups and saucers from the front room. She was followed by Julie who had got the bucket and sponges.

'Hi Tom,' Julie smiled. 'Mum's given us some sweets to keep us going,' she added, pointing to a bag on one of kitchen surfaces.

'Oh thanks, Mrs Martin,' said Tom. 'It seems ages since breakfast already!'

'Just behave yourselves, you two. And make sure you wear your wellies, Julie. I don't want you coming back with soaking feet!' Mrs Martin warned.

'You'd better start with our car first,' said Julie's dad, 'That will give you something to practise on!'

'I'll bring the soapy water, Tom. You fix up the hose for rinsing the car when we've finished,' Julie said. She squirted some washing up liquid into the bucket and watched the suds foam up as the warm water ran into it from the tap.

Tom busied himself fixing one end of the hose

pipe to the cold tap. Scruff had sensed something unusual was happening and had come back into the kitchen to have a nose around. He pulled at the neatly rolled hose pipe. Before Tom had time to stop him, the kitchen floor had become a tangle of hose pipe with Scruff tugging and pulling in the middle of it all.

'Oh Scruff – you little terror! Come out at once,' shouted Mrs Martin. She grabbed hold of the dog's collar and tried to drag him away. But Scruff was reluctant to leave his newly discovered game. He hung on to his rubber 'snake' until Mr Martin came to the rescue and forced it out of his mouth.

'Into the back garden with you,' said Mr Martin, pushing Scruff out of the door. 'You're always causing chaos.'

Tom eventually found the end of the hose, untangled it, picked it up and stretched it out to the drive ready for later. Julie borrowed the kitchen stool to enable her to reach the top of the car and off they went.

They had just finished giving the car its soapy wash when Mrs Martin appeared with drinks and biscuits for 'the workers.'

'I could get to enjoy this sort of life,' thought Julie, munching her chocolate digestive. As she looked up, she noticed Scruff had appeared on the scene. He must have got out of the back garden when her mum had brought the drinks round. Scruff thought car washing looked like fun as

well, and was busy putting his paw into the
bucket, attracted by the soapy bubbles.

'Scruff! Come out at once!' Julie shouted at him.
Scruff withdrew his paw quickly. But as he did
so, he knocked over the bucket. Water splashed
all over him and the drive.

'Oh Scruff!'

Julie ran towards him to tell him off. But Scruff
thought she was playing a game. He grabbed one
of the water-filled sponges in his mouth, shook it
and ran. The water from the sponge showered
everywhere. Julie ducked behind the car to keep
dry. Tom saw his chance to grab Scruff round
the neck but Scruff slipped free, leaving Tom off
balance. He fell forwards into the soapy puddle

on the drive and soaked his jeans!

Scruff thought it was a great game and ran off, still clutching the sponge. Julie chased him, round and round the garden. At last she caught up with him and managed to wrestle the sponge away from his grasp.

'You bad dog!' she scolded and led him firmly into the back garden. This time she made sure that Scruff would not escape!

Tom picked himself up and rubbed himself down. He wasn't in too much of a state, and his jeans would soon dry in the sun. In fact he'd quite enjoyed the whole episode. Car washing was certainly not dull, that was for sure! Tom dried the car off and he stood back with Julie to admire the result of their handiwork.

'I reckon we've done a good job, don't you?' said Tom, looking at his reflection in the bonnet.

'Yep! My dad'll be pleased with that,' confirmed Julie.

The rest of the morning sped by without mishap. Tom's money box got heavier and heavier with the cash they had collected. It was now getting on for dinner time. Both Julie and Tom were feeling hungry but they still had one last car to do. Their keenness and enthusiasm had left them and tiredness had made them just a little careless. Julie had managed to get water down one of her wellingtons and every time she walked she squelched rather uncomfortably. One of Tom's

sleeves had come unrolled and had got soaking wet in the water.

'Not much more to do now, Tom,' said Julie as they finished washing down Mrs Gordon's mini.

'No – just the hosing down,' replied Tom. 'I'm glad, because I'm getting a bit fed up with it now, aren't you?'

'Yeah! My tum tells me I'm ready for my dinner! Still – just think of all the money we've raised. I bet we've collected more than £10,' Julie said.

'So do I – and it feels like it,' replied Tom, picking up the money box.

'We can count it after dinner and find out. Come on, let's get finished and go home. I'll just go and turn the tap on for the hose,' said Julie, disappearing into the house.

Tom fiddled with the hose pipe in a bored way, swinging it around this way and that. He certainly didn't expect the water to come shooting out of it! It shot out quicker than usual. The force of it made the hose pipe straighten up and jerk out of Tom's hand. It swirled round in the air and sent a stream of icy cold water straight at Julie just as she stepped out of the door. The water hit her straight in the face, making her draw her breath in sharply and step backwards.

'What . . . ?'

Unfortunately for Julie, the bucket of dirty soapy water was just behind her. In went her foot – and over she went with a thump – bucket, water and all. Water poured all over her, whilst the hose pipe writhed about uncontrollably. It sent jets of water over the drive and everything else in its path. What a mess!

Tom rushed to help Julie – and got a jet of water up the leg of his jeans from the hose pipe!

'Oh,' he shrieked as he let go of her again, allowing her to fall back into the soapy puddle for a second time.

From inside, Mrs Gordon could hear the commotion. 'What's going on?' she wondered, going towards the door. 'Oh dear me no!' she gasped with concern as she saw what had happened. She rushed back into the kitchen to turn off the tap. The jet of water from the hose pipe subsided into a trickle and finally stopped altogether. Julie spluttered and wailed, wet and cold as Tom eventually managed to pick her up.

'S . . s . . sorry Julie,' he stuttered. 'The hose pipe seemed to have a mind of its own. It just jumped out of my hand.'

Mrs Gordon wasn't quite sure whether to laugh at the funniness of the situation or cry at the mess. She took one look at Julie's expression and saw that she was near to tears.

'Come on you two,' she said kindly. 'Just leave this for a minute and come in and dry your-selves.'

Ten minutes later, Julie and Tom emerged from

the house feeling much better. They'd had a hot drink and had dried themselves as best they could with towels.

'Shall we try and finish the job?' asked Julie.

'OK' said Tom 'but this time *you* hold the hose and *I'll* go and turn the tap on.' They both managed a weak smile at this.

A quarter of an hour later, they had finished, and Julie was squelching uncomfortably down the street. Tom was trailing water behind him as it dripped down from his sodden jumper and plopped on the pavement. At the corner they separated.

'Come round later, Tom, and we'll count the money,' said Julie.

'OK, see you some time this afternoon,' said Tom.

As she walked home, Julie looked forward to her usual Saturday dinner of fish and chips. Her stomach rumbled with the thought of it. But she was also wondering how to explain about the state she'd got her clothes into.

As Tom walked home he felt a bit lonely. He wished he'd got a mum who would be there to make him lunch. Instead he'd have to make himself a sandwich or something. Still, the thought of the money in the box cheered him up. It felt quite heavy. 'I wonder how much we've collected. Maybe I'll count it while I eat my sandwich,' he thought.

Tom finished his cheese sandwich and emptied

his glass of squash. It was quiet in the flat. Tom began to feel lonely again. He picked up his comic but soon put it down again as he'd already read it twice. He got up and put on the TV. Ugh! Horse racing. Tom hated horse racing. It would'have been a different story if it had been motor racing or football. He punched the 'off' button in disgust and wandered about aimlessly, wondering what to do with himself. As he was walking past the shelf his eyes turned towards his metal money box. Tom went over and picked it up.

'Mmm. That's pretty heavy,' he thought. 'I bet there's quite a bit more than £10.'

Tom shook it and then put it down again. After all, he'd promised Julie that they'd count it together. He sat down again, but his mind kept going back to the money.

'Surely it won't matter if I count it first,' he thought to himself. 'It won't do any harm will it?'

Suddenly he'd decided. He got up again, picked up the key, and opened the lid. Tom tipped the money onto the floor. It cascaded and clinked as it showered onto the carpet forming a little money mountain. First Tom sorted out the pound coins. 'Eleven! Wow!' Next he turned to the silver. There were three fifty pence pieces, five twenties, two tens and three fives. £13.85 altogether. Tom got really excited. Would they beat the £14 mark he wondered. He gathered together all the copper coins. They totalled 20p so altogether they had earned £14.05. Tom gave a low whistle. 'Wow! That was some morning's work.'

Tom liked money. He spent several minutes putting it into different piles, picking it up, letting it trickle through his fingers. He fiddled with it, rolled the pound coins along the floor, spun the 50p coins in the air and flicked the copper coins like tiddlywinks.

'£14.05 – that's a lot more than you expected to collect,' a voice inside him seemed to say. 'It feels good, doesn't it? You've never had that much money of your own, have you?'

Tom looked at the pile of coins. It would be nice if they belonged to him.

But another voice inside his head was saying, 'Come on Tom. Put the money in the box now and take it round to Julie's.'

'Don't be so silly, Tom,' answered the first voice. 'You've got plenty of time. Enjoy playing with the money for a bit longer.'

Tom looked around. He felt as if he was being watched. He felt a bit uncomfortable. He began to get the money together, ready to put it back in the box.

'Oh come on Tom. There's no need to do that yet. Hey! Julie doesn't know how much you collected does she? She'd never miss a pound would she? That would still leave £13.05 and that's more than she's expecting. You earned it, didn't you? You worked hard for it, didn't you?

Nobody would ever know. Go on Tom, take a pound for your effort. You could get yourself something really good for a pound. Take it now. Put it in your pocket.'

Tom felt hot and sweaty. It was hard to ignore the voice. He knew it was wrong – but did it really matter? Would anyone find out? And it wouldn't hurt anyone would it? Tom's hand reached out. It hovered over the pile of money.

Tom's got a problem.
Make a spinner to decide what he will do.
Trace this shape on to thin card. Draw in the numbers and cut it out. Push a used matchstick through the centre. Now spin the spinner.

If it lands on 1 or 2, read the ending on page 64.
If it lands on 3 or 4, read the ending on page 65.
If it lands on 5 or 6, read the ending on page 67.
(But you can always read the other endings later!)

Tom's mind was a battlefield. Half of him wanted to take the money. Half of him knew it was wrong.

The pile of coins on the carpet glinted at him, tempting him. It would be so easy to take a pound.

Tom had to do something. He couldn't just leave the money there. He sat down and grabbed a handful of coins. The money clattered as he threw it into the box. He picked up the rest and tipped that into the box too. As he did so, a pound coin hit the edge and rolled away on the carpet. It spun for a few seconds, wobbled and then settled. It lay there, mocking him, inviting him to pick it up and pocket it.

The battle raged on in Tom's head. Tom looked at the coin and it seemed to look back at him, challenging him. Suddenly, with a snatch, Tom grabbed it. His hand lingered near his pocket for a moment. Then with a real effort of will, Tom threw the coin into the box, slammed the lid and turned the key.

Quickly he put on his coat and hurried out of the flat. Slamming the door behind him, Tom ran all the way to Julie's. He didn't want time to stop and think in case he changed his mind.

'Hello Tom! What have you been up to? You're all red and out of breath,' said Julie as she answered the door.

'Oh nothing much,' mumbled Tom. 'I've just been running that's all. Come on—let's count this money.'

Tom felt funny all over. His head spun as the voices battled in his mind. Should he take the money or not?

Tom's hand seemed to have a mind of its own. It didn't seem to belong to him anymore. It dipped into the box. His fingers closed around a pound coin, drew it out and slipped it into his pocket. Tom's palm felt clammy and sticky. His heart seemed to be beating faster and louder. Tom watched his hand as it shut the lid of the box and turned the key.

A few moments later, Tom had his coat on and was walking out of the flat towards Julie's. His feet seemed to be walking slower than usual. Tom hardly noticed where he was going. His mind was racing. The pound coin seemed to be burning a hole in his pocket. Tom's fingers closed round it. The metal box was heavy in his other hand.

The two voices were still arguing inside him. They just would not keep quiet.

'Walk quicker, Tom, before you change your mind. You can spend the pound on the way home,' said the one voice.

'Tom – put the money back – it doesn't belong to you,' said the other.

Before he knew it Tom found himself at Julie's gate. But Tom hesitated. His feet were like lead. It was as if he was glued to the spot.

'I can't do it,' he thought.

He suddenly realized what he was about to do.

He was about to steal food from the mouths of starving children. It was no good. He couldn't go ahead with it.

Suddenly Tom took the coin from his pocket and dropped it into the box. He felt quite sick at the thought of what he'd almost done.

'Hallo Tom! What have you been up to? You look a bit odd,' said Julie as she opened the door, to him.

'Oh do I? I must have been hurrying to get here I suppose. And I was doing some thinking. Come on – let's get counting the money.'

Without further thought Tom grabbed a pound coin and put it straight in his pocket. He gathered up the rest of the money and put it into the money box. He slammed the lid and locked it.

Minutes later, Tom was walking down the street towards Julie's, carrying the money box containing just £13.05.

As he passed Swindons, the newsagents on the corner, his feet seemed to take him in. Tom looked at the display of sweets and chocolates and worked out what he could get for a pound.

Tom blinked hard. He didn't feel quite right. He felt hot and dizzy.

'Are you alright, Tom?' Mr Swindon asked. 'You look a bit pale today.'

'Yes, I'm OK, thanks,' stammered Tom.

'What can I do for you then?'

'I'll have these please.'

Tom handed over some sweets.

'That'll be 75p, please.'

Tom handed over the pound coin.

'You must have won the football pools,' joked the shopkeeper, 'You don't normally spend as much as that.'

Tom forced a smile and took the change guiltily. It was strange, but his hands were all clammy. He was glad to get out of the shop. He stood on the pavement and unwrapped a bar of chocolate.

Suddenly he didn't feel at all like eating. The chocolate seemed to stick to the roof of his mouth.

Tom couldn't swallow it. Just then a picture of the starving children flashed into his mind. They were dying because they didn't have enough to eat. Tom pushed the picture out of his head. He stuffed the chocolate into his pocket and strode on towards Julie's. Tom's mind was in a turmoil.

He knew he'd done wrong. It made him feel quite sick and dizzy. Tom walked to Julie's in a blur. His stomach was churning.

Suddenly Tom realized he had reached Julie's. He hadn't taken much notice of the journey because of his racing thoughts. There was Julie – standing at the door – smiling – waiting for him.

'Hello Tom! What have you been up to?'

Tom felt guilty. Julie couldn't know, could she?

'Oh . . . nothing' stuttered Tom.

'Come on in – let's count up the money' said Julie.

Tom thrust the tin into Julie's hand.

'You do it Julie. I'm not feeling very well. I'm going home.'

With that, Tom turned and ran down the path. The chocolate seemed heavy and bulky in his pocket. He couldn't take the half-eaten bar back. He knew what he'd done was stealing. He'd just have to hope no one ever found out.

7

Lucy and Sally's Saturday morning was going to be devoted to Odd Jobs Unlimited.

During the week, the girls had met together most evenings at each others houses to work out what they were going to do. First they made a list of all the people they knew – neighbours, friends and relatives.

'Right. Now we need to ask them what odd jobs we could do for them,' said Sally.

The rest of the week was spent talking to the people on their list. When the girls had explained that they were trying to raise money to help people in Africa who were suffering, most people seemed interested and found them jobs they could do. Everyone's name was written down and Lucy worked out a time table for Saturday.

By 9 o'clock on Saturday morning Lucy was ringing Sally's bell. She was carrying a special plastic bank bag to keep their earnings in. It already contained a pound coin she'd got from her parents for cleaning her bedroom.

'Cor, you look good,' said Lucy as Sally opened the door. Sally was wearing trainers, jeans and an old sweatshirt. She'd used some fluorescent coloured felt tips to print 'Odd Jobs Unlimited' in big bold letters on it, just to make sure everyone knew what they were doing. She reckoned that those who didn't know what it meant would ask her. That would give her a chance to explain about the Gang's project.

'Come on, what's first?' asked Sally.

Mr and Mrs Robinson were top of the list. They just wanted a bit of shopping done.

'That was easy,' laughed Lucy. 'I hope the rest are the same!' The girls walked on to the Scotts. Mr Scott wasn't keen on gardening so he was glad of their help.

'I'll mow the lawns while you weed the borders and trim the edges,' he said. He chatted away to them as they were working and told them how much he supported their idea.

'It's a pity more young people don't make an effort,' he said. 'The world would be a lot better if everyone thought like you.' The girls felt really pleased and told him more about Quest Club and its activities.

'I wish I'd had something like that when I was at school,' he said when they'd finished.

Just as they finished the border, Mrs Scott brought out some orange squash and chocolate biscuits. 'I thought you'd like some elevenses before you move on,' she said.

Their next few calls were fairly uneventful. They included peeling potatoes, hanging out washing and walking a dog. But they all meant that the plastic bank bag began to bulge reassuringly with money they'd earned. Lucy and Sally were really enjoying themselves. As well as earning money for a good cause they were helping others at the same time.

Mrs Archer lived in an old house with peeling paintwork. It was set back off the road. The house looked dark and uncared for. The garden was wild and overgrown.

Sally glanced at Lucy as they approached the house.

'Doesn't it look creepy? Joanne Biggs says Mrs Archer's really strange. She says she's seen her through whe window cooking funny things. And she was talking to herself,' Lucy said.

'I've only seen her once,' Sally replied. 'She was all in black and sort of bent over when she walked, too.'

The girls stood at the broken gate. They stared hard at the house, trying to see through the windows.

'Look! The curtains moved,' Sally cried with a start.

'It's creepy. I don't fancy going in, do you?' asked Lucy. She clutched Sally's arm tightly. Sally tried to sound brave but her heart was pounding as she replied.

'Not really – but Mum says all these tales about her are nonsense. She's just a lonely old lady. And anyway Mum promised that we'd call on her. Come on. We'll have to do it.'

The wooden gate squeaked on its rusty hinges as Sally pushed it open. Their hearts beat faster as they approched the front door with its tarnished brass door knocker.

The girls heard the knock echo eerily in the emptiness. There was no other sound from within. Lucy was tempted to leave straight away but Sally restrained her.

'Come on – we can't go now. Listen I can hear something!' There was a shuffling noise and the sound of a key turning. Sally and Lucy looked at each other their eyes wide with worry. The door creaked open and there stood Mrs Archer.

'You must be Sally and Lucy,' came her quavering voice. 'How lovely of you to come and see me! Your mum said you would come and call. Come in.'

Standing in the doorway of her house, Mrs Archer didn't look frightening at all. She was just a frail old lady, rather small and wrinkled and quite harmless. Her dark eyes had a twinkle in them as she smiled in welcome and invited the girls in.

Sally and Lucy looked at each other again in relief as they followed Mrs Archer into her front room.

There was a musty smell about the house which came from old age and neglect. The wallpaper had faded to yellow. The room was darkened by the curtains which were still tightly pulled. A fat sleek black cat looked up lazily from its comfortable cushion. It decided that the interruption was not worth worrying about and promptly settled down to sleep again.

'Now come on Jack! That's no way to treat visitors,' Mrs Archer said to her pet, tipping him off the cushion. He meowed in protest but was soon purring like a traction engine as Lucy stroked him. He arched his back with pleasure.

'Sit you down, sit you down,' said Mrs Archer ushering them to the settee. 'It's lovely to see you, dears. I get so few visitors these days. Now tell me all about yourselves and what you're up to.'

The old lady settled herself comfortably in an armchair and smiled warmly at them both.

Any fear of Mrs Archer melted away as this gentle old lady sat and stroked Jack, who jumped up on to her lap the moment she sat down. Lucy and Sally took turns to explain why they were doing 'Odd Jobs Unlimited.' As Mrs Archer nodded and listened, she picked up her knitting from a nearby table. The needles clicked in accompaniment to Lucy and Sally's talk. When they had finished Mrs Archer put down her knitting and smiled once more.

'Why – I think that's a wonderful idea. I wish I could help you in some way but it isn't easy when you're old. I only have my pension you see.'

As Lucy carried on talking, Sally's mind was working overtime. Something was nagging at the back of her brain and she couldn't remember what it was. She forced her mind to think back over the Gang's discussions. Money was certainly one way to help but . . . suddenly it came! That was it! Mr Crossland had been talking about Mrs Crossland knitting things for Africa. They needed woollen blankets and vests to keep warm at night. And Mrs Archer was good at knitting!

'But you *can* help!' blurted out Sally. Lucy looked at her in amazement. She had been halfway through a sentence when Sally had suddenly burst in.

'Oh, sorry Lucy! I didn't mean to interrupt,' apologized Sally.

'Oh, that's OK. You carry on Sally – you've obviously had a brainstorm of some sort. It looks like you'll pop with excitement if you don't say what's on your mind!' exclaimed Lucy.

Sally thoughts tumbled out as she explained about the woollen blankets and vests. 'Well, I certainly enjoy knitting,' said Mrs Archer. 'Do you girls think you could collect odd balls of wool and find me a pattern?'

'Oh yes,' answered Sally, 'And we could come round and see you again with them.'

'I think I'd like that very much,' smiled Mrs Archer. 'After all,' she added, 'I've got lots of time and nothing much to do.'

'We'd better go now,' explained Lucy, 'We've still got another visit to make.' Mrs Archer was sorry to see them leave.

'I've enjoyed meeting you, girls,' she said. 'And I'll look forward to being able to make vests for the children.'

As the girls walked down the path they looked back. 'How on earth could we have been worried about a kind lonely old lady?' asked Sally.

They made up their minds to visit her regularly. Perhaps raising money wasn't the most important thing!

'Who's last then?' asked Sally, as they walked down Middleton Avenue. They stopped as Lucy checked the list. There was only one name left – the rest had been ticked off as they'd done them.

'It's number 42', said Lucy. 'Mrs Pearson'.

'Oh, her little boy's called Jason, isn't he? He's really funny,' said Sally.

'He looks a bit of a handful to me,' said Lucy.

They walked up the path of 42 Middleton Avenue. But even before they got to the door they could hear Jason crying loudly. Mrs Pearson answered their knock. Her blonde hair was ruffled and her face looked strained.

'Oh, hello girls. Thank goodness you've come. I'm having a terrible morning. Jason's teething and irritable and on top of that he's just fallen over. I've got the house to clean, the washing to hang out, and the ironing to do. And it's nearly Jason's dinner time as well.'

Lucy was surprised to see that Mrs Pearson was near to tears and in a bit of a state. Jason's screaming pierced the air. Each time he shrieked, Mrs Pearson winced and closed her eyes as if she had a splitting headache. She looked as if she was about to crumple. The only way Lucy could think of helping at that moment was to stop Jason crying.

'Here – let's take Jason into the garden and play with him for a bit,' suggested Lucy. 'It'll give you time to get a few things done'.

'Oh, would you? Thanks. That would be a real help,' replied Mrs Pearson, smiling weakly, dragging her hand through her hair in a worried way.

When they went in the girls were shocked to see the house in such state. Jason's toys were scattered everywhere. The settee was stacked with piles of ironing and there was a mountain of dirty washing-up in the sink. Jason was sitting in the middle of this chaos howling. He stopped for a moment when he saw the girls.

Lucy bent down to pick him up. 'Come on', she said. 'What's the matter? I bet you want to play don't you?'

She whirled him round in her arms and took
him off into the gardens. The fresh air and change
of scenery worked wonders. Suddenly, he was the
centre of attention. He sniffed and rubbed his
eyes.

Sally called out to him, and then ducked behind
a tree. She waited until Jason looked around for
her before poking her head out. 'Boo!' she
exclaimed. Jason gave a throaty chuckle and
clapped his hands. His mood had changed
completely.

Out of the corner of her eye Lucy noticed Mrs
Pearson staring anxiously through the window.

'Do you think she's alright?' Lucy asked Sally.
'Where's Mr Pearson?'

'I don't know', answered Sally. 'Do you think I should go in and help her tidy up a bit?'

'That's a good idea. I'll stay out here and keep Jason occupied.'

Sally went into the kitchen, where Mrs Pearson was beginning to make a half-hearted attempt to do the washing-up. 'Shall I help pick up Jason's toys for you?' asked Sally.

'I'm glad you two came. I seem to be in a real mess this morning don't I?'.

'Oh you ought to see our house sometimes,' said Sally. 'Anyway, Jason seems fine now – look.' They looked out of the window to see Lucy throwing a big plastic ball to Jason, who was laughing and shouting happily.

Sally felt sorry for Mrs Pearson. She looked so sad and everything seemed to be getting on top of her. Sally set about cleaning up the mess in the front room and in no time at all it looked a lot better. Jason's toys went into a big box and the papers and magazines were put into tidy piles.

Next Sally helped dry the crockery which Mrs Pearson had washed up. Mrs Pearson talked and talked and talked. Sally didn't really understand most of the things but somehow it seemed to be helping Mrs Pearson. She was relaxing and beginning to unwind. Once the hoovering had been done, she even smiled.

Just as Mrs Pearson was putting the vacuum cleaner away, Lucy came in with Jason. He was much more cheerful now and made straight for his toy box.

'I'll get his dinner ready,' said Mrs Pearson. 'Would you like to stay a bit longer – I'd love you to.'

Lucy looked at her watch. It was 12.30 and getting on for their lunch-time. 'We'd better call home to make sure that's all right,' she said.

After the phone-calls, the girls stayed and helped give Jason his dinner. Sally was quite excited at feeding him as she'd never done anything like that before.

'I don't know how to thank you girls enough', she said. 'Will you come to see us again? Jason doesn't get many visitors to play with.'

Jason gurgled and carried on chewing his crust, ignoring his mum.

'Yes, of course,' replied Lucy. 'We'd love to take Jason for a walk sometime.'

Mrs Pearson carried Jason to the door to wave goodbye. She was a lot calmer now than when they had arrived. The house was hardly recognizable from an hour or so before.

'Bye Jason' they chorused from the door. Jason looked up, smiled and gurgled.

Mrs Pearson stood at the door and watched the girls walk down the path and along the road until they were out of sight.

'I never thought that grown-ups had problems,' said Lucy, as they walked home. Meeting Mrs

Pearson had made them think. They began to realize that it wasn't just people in other parts of the world who had bad problems. First there was Mrs Archer and then Mrs Pearson who needed help in different ways.

'I'll come round to your house to count the money after lunch,' said Lucy to Sally as she turned to go down her street. Sally waved a hand in agreement and disappeared out of sight.

Over lunch, Lucy told her mum and dad all that had happened during the morning. 'I reckon you've done really well, both of you,' said Lucy's mum, 'I'm proud of you. I'm worried about Mrs Pearson though. I've seen her at church sometimes, but I didn't know she was in such a state. I'll call round and see if I can do anything to help.'

'That's a good idea,' agreed Lucy's dad, 'And I'll ask John what he knows about the situation.' (John was the minister of their church.)

'And don't forget about Mrs Archer either!'

'No! we won't forget her! She'll be on our visiting list too!' smiled Lucy's dad. 'From what you've said it sounds as if her garden's long overdue for some attention. And you know how much I love gardening!'

Everyone laughed at his joke. Lucy's dad disliked gardening as much as Mr Scott did. 'And Lucy – as you're so good at gardening now, I'm sure you'll be glad to give me a hand with it,' he joked.

Lucy grinned wryly and got on with her dinner. She'd asked for that one!

Vest Pattern

You will need: double knitting wool and number 8 needles

OR

4 ply wool and number 9 needles

Use any colour wool except white.

Cast on 60 stitches.

Rib (knit 1, purl 1) for 6 inches.

Cast off 4 stitches at the beginning of the next two rows.

Continue in rib for 2 more inches.

Rib for 16 stitches, cast off 20 stitches, rib for 16 stitches.

Rib on the last 16 stitches for 16 rows. Leave them on a spare needle.

Rejoin the wool to the other 16 stitches and rib for 16 rows.

Next row, rib 16 stitches, cast on 20 stitches, pick up and rib the 16 stitches on the spare needle.

Rib for 2 inches.

Cast on 4 stitches at the beginning of the next 2 rows.

Rib for 6 inches. Cast off.

Pick up 42 stitches for the sleeve. Rib for 8 rows. Cast off.

Work the other sleeve to match. Sew up the side seams.

When you have finished your vest, send it to:

ECHO
Ullswater Crescent
Coulsdon
Surrey
CR3 2HR

8

When Sunday afternoon came, the Quest Gang
were seated round Jake and Julie's kitchen table.
They had agreed to meet after lunch to pool the
money they had raised and discover the grand
total. Then they would have to decide what to do
with it.

As each pair counted out their money, Raju
made a note of the total. The money which he and
Jake had raised was the last to be counted. Their
contribution came to £13.45.

'How much does that make altogether?' asked
Lucy.

Raju flourished a pencil. On a piece of clean
paper he wrote:

Quest Gang's Campaign for Africa
Jake and Raju £13.45
Tom and Julie £14.05
Lucy and Sally £12.90

Raju cleared his throat ready to make the grand announcement. His face took on the look of a TV newscaster about to make a world-shattering statement.

'Oh come on Raju – get on with it. What's the total?' asked Sally, who was longing to know.

'Patience,' said Raju. He was enjoying every moment of being the focus of attention. He held up the paper in front of him and cleared his throat once more.

'It is my pleasure,' began Raju, in his best and poshest voice, 'to announce the result of the Quest Gang's fund-raising attempts to help Africa.' He paused for further effect, 'After much hard work and effort we have managed to raise the grand sum of £40.40.'

Almost before he'd finished, the Gang errupted into wild applause and jubilation. Whoops of joy were mixed with cries of 'I don't believe it!' and 'I never thought we'd make so much!' There was much leaping about, backslapping and hugging. Scruff added to the noise, barking and darting about from one gang member to another.

'What's all the excitement about?' asked Jake's dad as he poked his head around the door. He'd been dozing quietly in front of the TV only to be woken by the unexpected explosion of noise. 'Has someone won the football pools?' he asked.

The Gang all tried to tell him the good news at once, each trying to out do the other.

'Whoa! Slow down! One at a time,' he said.

As the babble subsided Jake explained how much they'd raised altogether.

'I'm proud of you all,' he smiled. 'Imagine doing all that on your own. I reckon government and adults ought to take a leaf out of your book. This deserves a celebration.' He looked back over his shoulder into the lounge and called to his wife. 'Have we got something special to mark the Gang's success?' he asked.

All eyes turned towards Julie's mum.

'I've got just the thing' she said with a smile. She made for the fridge and took out a large bottle of lemonade. There was a satisfying hiss of escaping gas as the top was loosened. The drink frothed and splashed, fizzing and bubbling to the very top of each glass.

In the meantime, Mr Martin had found some crisps and chocolate biscuits to make the celebration complete. The chattering turned into munching and gulping.

'Well – now what?' asked Julie's dad as they finished drinking. 'You need to find out what to do with the money so that it will be best used. An organization like Tear Fund would be able to help you.'

This was greeted with nods from round the table.

'Mr Crossland said he'd help us with that. We could talk to him tomorrow at Quest Club,' suggested Julie.

'Yeah – that's a good idea. And we can tell him all about our weekend. Perhaps we could do something about it for Harvest. After all, we have been raising money for food for the hungry,' said Jake.

Everyone seemed to be in general agreement. Jake's dad smiled and went back to watching TV. The Gang collected up the money, put it safely away and went outside to enjoy what was left of the warm September sun.

9

The next morning the Quest Gang could hardly wait to tell Mr Crossland of their exploits. They agreed to try and see him at morning break time.

'You've done all that this weekend?' asked Mr Crossland, when he managed to get a word in. He was quite surprised at everything they'd done in such a short space of time.

'Now, let me suggest what you could do with the money.' When he'd finished telling them about the work Tear Fund did throughout the world, the Gang all agreed that Tear Fund was where their money should go.

After school the Quest Club had its usual Monday meeting. Mr Crossland invited Mr Cansdale, the headmaster, to come along and hear what the Gang had been up to.

'Raju, perhaps you'd tell us what you've all been doing.'

'Well,' he began, 'It all started last week when we saw the famine pictures on TV. Then we remembered that the Quest Club meeting had been all about Jesus telling us we had to help people in need. And we thought we might be able to do something.'

At first Raju was nervous, but he soon warmed up. Everyone gasped when they heard how much had been raised. Raju stooped down and picked up his sports bag. He put it down with a thud on a nearby table.

'And this . . . ' he said, 'is what £40.40 looks like.' He tipped up his bag and out poured the money. The coins clattered onto the table with an impressive and satisfying crash. Everyone burst into spontaneous applause at the sight of it all. Mr Crossland was taken aback by the response.

Mr Cansdale spoke first.

'I think you'll all agree that Raju, Jake, Julie, Lucy, Sally and Tom have put a lot of thought, time and effort into their project. It just goes to show what can be done if you put your mind to it. I'm proud of you all,' he said as he smiled at them.

The Gang shuffled uncomfortably and looked down at their feet. The last few days had certainly been exciting. The Gang hadn't had time to think about much else. But they had enjoyed working together and helping other people. And it had been fun, too.

'Your example has given me a great idea of what we as a school can do about Harvest this year. Perhaps you could talk about your project in assembly tomorrow,' Mr Cansdale continued, looking at the six of them. He took Mr Crossland to one side and entered into a long conversation with him about his ideas.

The Gang were rapidly surrounded by the rest of the Quest Club, all clamouring to know more. When the meeting broke up at 5 o'clock the Gang felt tired but happy. They had all enjoyed every minute of the last week. And it wasn't over yet. Mr Cansdale was talking about a school-wide project!

The Quest Gang learn more about God by reading their Bibles with Quest. Why don't you join them! Quest has things to do, puzzles, codes and prayers. It's great with the Bible!

Write to the Quest Gang at your nearest Scripture Union office and ask them for a free Quest starter:

130 City Road, London EC1V 2NJ

9 Canal Street, Glasgow G4 0AB

12 Wellington Place, Belfast BT1 6GE

9 Northumberland Avenue, Dun Laoghaire, Co Dublin, Eire

or your national Scripture Union Office.